12.95

{ INTERIM SITE }

S0-BNQ-704

3 1192 00472 4819

x398/G88ha

Grimm, Jacob, 1785-1863.

Hansel and Gretel

HANSEL AND GRETEL

STORY BY THE BROTHERS GRIMM
ILLUSTRATIONS BY ARNOLD LOBEL

DELACORTE PRESS / SEYMOUR LAWRENCE

EVANSTON PUBLIC LIBRARY
CHILDREN'S DEPARTMENT
1703 ORRINGTON AVENUE
EVANSTON, ILLINOIS 60201

Published by
Delacorte Press/Seymour Lawrence
1 Dag Hammarskjold Plaza
New York, N.Y. 10017

Copyright © 1971 by Arnold Lobel

All rights reserved. No part of this book may be reproduced or
transmitted in any form or by any means, electronic or mechanical,
including photocopying, recording, or by any information storage
and retrieval system, without the written permission of the
Publisher, except where permitted by law.

Manufactured in the United States of America

One Previous Edition

New Edition
First printing—May 1985

Library of Congress Cataloging in Publication Data
The Library of Congress has cataloged the first
printing of this title as follows:
Grimm, Jakob Ludwig Karl, 1785–1863.
Hansel and Gretel.   Story by the brothers Grimm.   Illus.
by Arnold Lobel.   New York, Delacorte Press [1971]
37 p.   col. illus.   19 x 22 cm. $3.95
A retelling of the adventures of a brother and sister left in the
woods by their wicked stepmother.
[1. Fairy tales]   I. Grimm, Wilhelm Karl, 1786–1859, joint
author.   II. Lobel, Arnold, illus.   III. Title.
PZ8.G882Ha 30   398.22   75–117296
ISBN 0-385-28387-3   MARC
Library of Congress   71 [4]   A C

TO MICHAEL AND HEATHER

HANSEL AND GRETEL

ONCE UPON A TIME there dwelt on the outskirts of a large forest a poor woodcutter with his wife and two children; the boy was called Hansel, and the girl Gretel. He had always little enough to live on, and once, when there was a great famine in the land, he couldn't even provide them with daily bread.

One night, as he was tossing about in bed, full of cares and

worry, he sighed and said to his wife, "What's to become of us? How are we to feed our poor children, when we have nothing more for ourselves?"

"I'll tell you what, husband," answered the woman. "Early tomorrow morning we'll take the children out into the thickest part of the wood. There we shall light a fire for them and give them each a piece of bread. Then we'll go on to our work and leave them alone. They won't be able to find their way home, and we shall thus be rid of them."

"No, wife," said her husband, "that I won't do. How could I find it in my heart to leave my children alone in the wood? The wild beasts would soon come and tear them to pieces."

"Oh, you fool," said she, "then we must all four die of hunger,

and you may just as well go and plane the boards for our coffins."
And she left him no peace until he consented.

"But I can't help feeling sorry for the poor children," added
the husband.

The children, too, had not been able to sleep for hunger and
had heard what their step-mother had said to their father. Gretel
wept bitterly.

"Now all is over with us."

"No, no, Gretel," said Hansel, "don't worry. I'll find a way
out, no fear."

And when the old people had fallen asleep he got up, slipped
on his little coat, opened the back door, and stole out. The moon
was shining clearly, and the white peb-
bles which lay in front of the house glit-
tered like bits of silver. Hansel bent
down and filled his pocket with as many
of them as he could cram in. Then he

went back and said to Gretel, "Be comforted, my dear little sister, and go to sleep," and he lay down in bed again.

At daybreak, even before the sun was up, the woman came and woke the two children.

"Get up, lazybones, we're all going to the forest to fetch wood."

She gave them each a bit of bread and said, "There's something for your lunch, but don't eat it up before, for it's all you'll get."

Gretel put the bread in her apron, as Hansel had the stones in his pocket. Then they all set out together on the way to the forest.

After they had walked for a little, Hansel kept stopping to look back at the house. His father saw him and said, "Hansel, what are you looking at, and why do you always lag behind? Take care, and remember to use your legs."

"Oh, father," said Hansel, "I am looking back at my white kitten, which is sitting on the roof waving me a farewell."

The woman exclaimed, "What a donkey you are! That isn't your kitten, that's the morning sun shining on the chimney."

But Hansel had not looked back at his kitten. Each time he stopped he dropped one of the white pebbles out of his pocket onto the path.

When they had reached the middle of the forest the father said, "Now, children, go and fetch a lot of wood, and I'll light a fire so that you won't be cold."

Hansel and Gretel heaped up brushwood until they had made a pile nearly the size of a small hill. The brushwood was set on fire, and when the flames leaped high the woman said, "Now lie down at the fire, children, and rest yourselves. We are going into the forest to cut down wood. When we've finished we'll come back to fetch you."

Hansel and Gretel sat down beside the fire, and at midday ate their little bits of bread. They heard the strokes of the axe, so they thought their father was quite near. But it was no axe

they heard, but a bough he had tied to a dead tree being blown about by the wind. And when they had sat for a long time their eyes closed with fatigue, and they fell fast asleep. When they awoke at last it was pitch dark. Gretel began to cry.

"How are we ever to get out of the wood?" she said.

Hansel comforted her. "Wait a bit," he said, "until the moon is up, and then we'll find our way sure enough."

And when the full moon had risen he took his sister by the hand and followed the pebbles, which shone like newly coined silver pieces, showing them the path. They walked all through the night, and at daybreak reached their father's house again. They knocked at the door, and when the woman opened it she exclaimed, "You naughty children, what a time you've slept in the wood! We thought you were never going to come back."

But the father rejoiced, for his conscience had reproached him for leaving his children behind by themselves.

Not long afterward there was again a great famine in the land, and the children heard their step-mother address their father thus in bed one night: "Everything is eaten up once more. We have only half a loaf in the house, and when that's done all is over with us. The children must be got rid of. We'll lead them deeper into the wood this time, so that they won't be able to find their way out again. There is no other way of saving ourselves."

The man's heart was heavy, and he thought, "Surely it would be better to share the last bite with one's children!" But his wife wouldn't listen to his arguments, and did nothing but scold and reproach him. If a man yields once he's done for; and so, because he had given in the first time, he was forced to do so the second.

But the children were awake and had heard the conversation. When the old people were asleep Hansel got up, wanting to go out and pick up pebbles again as he had done the first time. But the woman had barred the door, and Hansel couldn't get out. He consoled his little sister, saying, "Don't cry, Gretel, and sleep peacefully, for I will think of something to help us."

At early dawn the woman came and made the children get up. They received their bit of bread, but it was even smaller than the time before. On the way to the wood Hansel crumbled it in his pocket, and every few minutes he stood still and dropped a crumb on the ground.

"Hansel, what are you stopping and looking about you for?" asked the father.

"I'm looking back at my little pigeon, which is sitting on the roof waving me a farewell," answered Hansel.

"Fool!" said the wife. "That isn't your pigeon, it's the morning sun glittering on the chimney."

But Hansel gradually threw all his crumbs onto the path. The woman led the children still deeper into the forest, farther than they had ever been in their lives. Then a big fire was lit again, and the step-mother said, "Just sit down there, children, and if you're tired you can sleep a bit. We're going into the forest to cut down wood, and in the evening when we're finished we'll come back to fetch you."

At midday Gretel divided her bread with Hansel, for he had dropped his all along their path. Then they fell asleep, and evening passed away, but nobody came to the poor children. They didn't awake until it was pitch dark, and Hansel comforted his sister, saying, "Only wait, Gretel, until the moon rises; then we shall see the bread crumbs I scattered along the path. They will show us the way back to the house."

When the moon appeared they got up, but they found no crumbs, for the thousands of birds that fly about the woods and fields had picked them all up.

"Never mind," said Hansel to Gretel, "you'll see, we'll still find a way out." But all the same they did not. They wandered about the whole night and the next day, from morning until evening, but they could not find a path out of the wood. They were very hungry, too, for they had nothing to eat but a few berries they found growing on some bushes. And at last they were so tired that their legs refused to carry them any longer, so they lay down under a tree and fell fast asleep.

On the third morning after they had left their father's house, they set about their wandering again, but only got deeper and deeper into the wood, until at last they felt that if help did not come to them soon they must perish.

At midday they saw a beautiful little snow-white bird sitting on a branch, which sang so sweetly that they stopped still to listen to it. And when its song was finished it flapped its wings and flew on in front of them. They followed it to a little house, on the roof of which it perched; and when they came quite near they saw

that the cottage was made of bread and roofed with cakes, while the window was made of transparent sugar.

"We will set to work on that," said Hansel, "and have a regular feast. I'll eat a bit of the roof, and you, Gretel, can eat some of the window."

Hansel stretched up his hand and broke off a little bit of the roof to see what it was like, and Gretel went to the casement and began to nibble at it. Thereupon a shrill voice called out from the room inside:

Nibble, nibble, little mouse,
Who is nibbling at my house?

The children answered:

The wind, the wind,
The heaven-born wind.

And the children went on eating, undisturbed. Hansel, who liked the taste of the roof, tore down a big bit of it, while Gretel pushed out a whole round window-pane, and sat down the better to enjoy it. Suddenly the door opened, and an ancient woman leaning on a staff hobbled out. Hansel and Gretel were so terrified that they let what they had in their hands fall. But the old woman shook her head and said, "Oh ho! You dear children, who led you here? Just come in and stay with me. No harm shall come to you."

She took them both by the hand and led them into the house, and laid a most sumptuous dinner before them—milk and sugared pancakes, with apples and nuts. After they had finished, two beautiful little white beds were prepared for them, and when Hansel and Gretel lay down in them they felt as if they were in heaven.

The old woman had appeared to be most friendly, but she was really an old witch who had misled the children, and had only built the little bread house in order to lure them in. When anyone came into her power she cooked and ate him, and held a regular feast day for the occasion. Now, witches have red eyes and cannot see far, but, like beasts, they have a keen sense of smell and know when human beings pass by. When Hansel and Gretel fell into her hands she laughed maliciously and said jeeringly, "I've got them now. They won't escape me."

Early in the morning, before the children were awake, she rose up, and when she saw them both sleeping so peacefully, with their round rosy cheeks, she muttered to herself, "That'll be a dainty mouthful!"

Then she seized Hansel with her bony hand and carried him into a little stable, and barred the door on him. He might scream as much as he liked, it did him no good.

Then she went to Gretel, shook her until she awoke, and cried, "Get up, lazybones, fetch water and cook something for your brother. When he's fat I'll eat him up."

Gretel began to cry bitterly. But it was no use. She had to do what the wicked witch commanded. So the best food was cooked for poor Hansel, but Gretel got only crab shells.

Every morning the old woman hobbled out to the stable and cried, "Hansel, put out your finger so that I may feel if you are getting fat."

But Hansel always stretched out a bone, and the old woman, whose eyes were dim, couldn't see it, and thinking always it was

Hansel's finger, wondered why he fattened so slowly. When four weeks passed and Hansel still remained thin, she lost patience and determined to wait no longer.

"Now then, Gretel," she called to the girl, "be quick and get some water. Hansel may be fat or thin, I'm going to cook him tomorrow."

Oh! How the poor little sister sobbed as she carried the water, and how the tears rolled down her cheeks!

"If only the wild beasts in the wood had eaten us," she cried, "then at least we should have died together."

"Just hold your peace," said the old hag. "It won't help you."

Early in the morning Gretel had to make the fire and put the kettle on to boil.

"First we'll bake," said the old dame. "I've heated the oven already and kneaded the dough."

She pushed Gretel out to the oven, from which fiery flames were already issuing.

"Creep in," said the witch, "and see if it's properly heated, so that we can put in the bread."

And once Gretel was inside, she intended to shut the oven and let her bake in it, and then she would eat her, too. But Gretel saw what she had in mind and said, "I do not know how I am to do it. How do I get in?"

"You silly goose!" said the hag. "The opening is big enough. See, I could get in myself," and she crawled toward it and poked her head into the oven. Then Gretel gave her a shove that sent her right in, shut the iron door, and drew the bolt. Gracious! How she yelled! It was quite horrible. But Gretel fled, and the wretched old woman was left to perish miserably.

Gretel flew straight to Hansel, opened the little stable door, and cried, "Hansel, we are free! The old witch is dead!"

Then Hansel sprang like a bird out of a cage when the door is opened. How they rejoiced, and embraced each other, and jumped for joy, and kissed one another! And as they had no longer any cause for fear, they went into the old hag's house, and there they found, in every corner of the room, boxes with pearls and precious stones.

"These are even better than pebbles," said Hansel, and crammed his pockets full of them.

Gretel said, "I, too, will bring something home," and she filled her apron full.

"But now," said Hansel, "let's go and get well away from the witch's wood."

When they had wandered about for some hours they came to a big lake.

"We can't get over," said Hansel. "I see no bridge or stepping-stones of any sort."

"Yes, and there's no ferryboat either," answered Gretel. "But

look, there swims a white duck. If I ask her, she'll help us over,"
and she called out:

> *Duck, duck, here we stand,*
> *Hansel and Gretel, on the land,*
> *Stepping-stones and bridge we lack,*
> *Carry us over on your nice white back.*

The duck swam toward them, and Hansel got on her back and bade his little sister sit beside him.

"No," answered Gretel, "we should be too heavy a load for the duck. She shall carry us across separately."

The good bird did this, and when they were landed safely on the other side, and had gone on for a while, the wood became more and more familiar to them, and at length they saw their father's house in the distance. Then they set off at a run, and bounding into the room, threw themselves round their father's neck. The man had not passed a happy hour since he left them in the wood, but the woman had died.

Gretel shook out her apron so that the pearls and precious stones rolled about the room, and Hansel threw down one handful after the other out of his pocket. Thus, all their troubles were ended, and they all lived happily ever after.

THE END